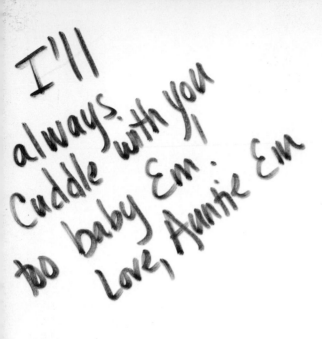

I'll always cuddle with you too baby Em.
Love, Auntie Em

The Cuddliest Cuddle in the World

The Cuddliest Cuddle in the World

Written by Sarah Nash
Illustrated by Daniel Howarth

PaRRagon

Bath · New York · Singapore · Hong Kong · Cologne · Delhi
Melbourne · Amsterdam · Johannesburg · Auckland · Shenzhen

Mommy's gone hunting. Leopard is
left at home. Leopard is feeling lonely.
He misses Mommy and he
misses Mommy's cuddles.

"What's up, Spottychops?" says Bear.
"No Mommy," whispers Leopard sadly.
"How about a hug to cheer you up?" suggests Bear.

"AAAA...OUUCHHH...GET off," chokes Leopard.
"Your...hugs are muuchhh too tight!"

"Sssshall I give you a
ssssqueeze," hisses Python.

"Stop it . . ." giggles Leopard. "Your cuddles are much too tickly."

"Climb up here for a snuggle,"
calls Monkey.
"Help . . . let me goooo . . ."
screams Leopard. "Your cuddles
are much too whooshy!"

"Sha . . . ha . . . ha . . . ll I give you
a cu . . . hu . . . huddle?" chuckles
Hyena.

"Yuck!" splutters Leopard.
"Your cuddles are too licky."

"I will embrace you . . ."
smiles Crocodile.
"Ouch . . ." yelps Leopard.
"Your cuddles are
so snappy."

"Can I give you a huglet?" whispers Spider.
"Oh no . . ." smiles Leopard.
"Your cuddles are way too small."

"Oh dear," sighs Leopard, "I do miss Mommy."

"Listen up, Leopard,"
cries everyone,
"Mommy's back."

"Hello, little Leopard," says Mommy,
"did you miss me?"
"Mmmmm . . . and your cuddles . . ."
sighs Leopard.

"You give the cuddliest cuddles
in the world!"

To Edward and Poppy
S. N.

For my wife Heidi –
your love and cuddles keep me strong
D. H.

Text copyright © Sarah Nash 2005
Illustrations copyright © Daniel Howarth 2005

This edition published by Parragon in 2011

Parragon
Queen Street House
4 Queen Street
Bath BA1 1HE, UK

Published by arrangement with Meadowside Children's Books
185 Fleet Street London EC4A 2HS

ISBN 978-1-4454-2204-6

Printed in China